TIGER TAKE OFF YOUR HAT

Penelope
Stewart
Tyrone
Whitney
Marshmallow
Tuffy
Tiger
Agnes

"THE LITTLE TWIRPS"

By
Linda P. Silbert
Alvin J. Silbert, Ed. D.

LITTLE TWIRPS ® Trademark Reg. U.S. Pat. Off.
ISBN 0-89544-051-2

Silbert & Bress Publications • Mahopac, N.Y. 10541

Hi. I'm Tiger. I wear big hats. I wear big hats because I like them.

I like them very much!

2

This really big hat is the one I like the most. I wear it almost all the

time. I even wear it when I play baseball.

My friends used to get mad about this. That is, everybody but

Whitney got mad. The others thought I couldn't see when I had it on.

4

They kept calling, "Tiger! Take off that hat! You can't see what you're doing!"

I would tell them, "I CAN see!" But they didn't think I could. This made me mad. I knew I could see.

What made me really mad was that I don't like them telling me what to do. I don't tell them what to do -- so I don't want them telling me what to do.

Let me tell you about our last baseball game. It changed my whole life.

Our side was up. I was up at bat. The pitcher threw. I swung. I missed.

"Strike One!" called the umpire.

The pitcher threw again. I swung again.

"Strike Two!" called the umpire.

The third pitch came. I swung so hard I turned all the way around.

"Strike three!" called the umpire.

Then my friends yelled, "Tiger! Take off that hat. You can't see what you're doing."

"I CAN see," I said. "And besides, everybody strikes out sometimes."

Then the other team was up at bat. The first batter hit a long fly. I yelled, "I'll get it!" I had to run very fast. I put my head down so I could run faster. I ran and ran.

I ran so fast, I ran right past the ball.

Then I heard a loud "THUD!" as the ball hit the ground behind me.

"You missed it," yelled my friends. "Take off that hat! You can't see what you're doing!"

16

"I CAN see!" I said. "Everybody misses a catch sometimes."

The game went on. The other team made three runs. They were
winning 3 - 0. Then we were up again. First thing, Tuffy hit a
homerun!

18

Then Stewart hit a homerun!

19

And Agnes hit a homerun!

20

Then I was up. Everybody was looking at me. I wanted to hit a
homerun too!

The pitcher threw. I swung. I missed. He threw again. I swung. I missed.

Then I heard, "Tiger take off that hat!"

I didn't say anything that time. But I was getting mad. The pitcher

threw again. I swung hard -- very hard.

23

I HIT it! What a hit! I started to run. I put my head down and I ran!

24

I ran right into the first baseman. I fell down.

I got up. I started to run again. I stepped on second. I kept running.

Then I tripped over third base.

I fell.

I rolled over twice.

But that didn't stop me. I got up. I kept running. I was sure home plate was right in front of me -- just two more steps and a slide. But I missed the plate. I was out.

That's when they told me to take off my hat or sit on the bench. I wouldn't take off my hat --

so -- I sat on the bench!

I was really mad. Next chance I got I was going to show them, I told myself.

My big chance came later. Whitney caught a fly ball, but he hurt himself doing it. He tripped and scraped his leg.

He sat down next to me. He told me to take his place. At first I was happy. Then I said to him "OK, but -- "

"But what?" he asked.

"I'm afraid that they will yell at me again," I said. Then Whitney made me feel better.

He said, "Tiger, I know you can play with that hat on. You know you can play with that hat on. Go show them."

It was nearly the end of the game. We were now ahead, but the other side still had one more out to go.

The next batter hit a high ball. We had to catch it to win the game.

Everyone started running for it. But no one could see it -- the sun was in their eyes.

Agnes ran into Tuffy. Tyrone fell over Stewart.

Penelope tripped over a rock.

But I could see the ball! I started running. I ran and ran. Then I jumped for it. I caught it!

We won!

All my friends ran over to me.

"That was a great catch!" they all said. "We won and you helped us!"

Then they wanted to know how I could see the ball.

"Easy," I told them. "My hat kept the sun out of my eyes."

And you know what --

they never told me to take off my hat again.